To the wonderful Milner family:
Joe, Lucy, Jonathan, Cary, (Clifford), Owen, Errol,
Benjamin, Margie, Rosabelle, Cooper, Peter, Anna,
Josie and Silas. I 'take my hat off' to them for
their dear friendship and for giving me some of
the happiest days of my life!

Neil x

Red Robin Books is an imprint of Corner To Learn Limited

Published by

Corner To Learn Limited
Willow Cottage • 26 Purton Stoke • Swindon • Wiltshire SN5 4JF • UK

ISBN: 978-1-905434-83-1

First published in the UK 2011
Text © Neil Griffiths 2011
Illustrations © Janette Louden 2011

Design by
David Rose

Printed in China

Hats off!

Neil Griffiths

Illustrated by Janette Louden

I wonder if you ever thought,
Just how many hats you might have bought.
Does a hat look good on your head?
Or do you like to go bare instead?

How many hats
do you really wear?
Well, try some of
these if you dare!

Hats too **big**, too tight
and **too** small,
Hats that just shouldn't
be worn at all!

Stiff hats worn by
chefs when they cook,
Hats so awful they
make everyone look!

Scarecrow hats made of straw,
Hats too wide to get through the door!

Pointed hats for
a posh princess,
Tartan cloth hats to
search Loch Ness!

Hats worn by dancers,
piled with fruit,
Tough hats needed
when you parachute!

Stretchy hats for
the swimming pool,
Hanky-type hats to
keep granddad cool!

Hats worn by astronauts
out in space,
Flashy helmets needed
to win a race!

Miners' hats with very bright lights,
Armoured hats that protect brave knights!

Hats worn by bishops as they pray,
Santa's hat he wears on his sleigh!

Wizards' hats for magic spells,
Jesters' hats with those silly bells!

Hats that are worn
to fight a fire,
White flat caps for
a cricket umpire!

Top hats worn in the circus ring,
Priceless hats worn by
a queen and king.

Hats for marching whilst on parade,
Mexican hats when you need some shade!

Hats for jolly pirates out at sea,
Students' hats to collect a degree!

Tough hats worn when out horse-riding,
Camouflaged hats just great for hiding!

Hats for Easter, full of flowers,
Homemade hats that took
you hours and hours!

Smart peaked hats for our bus drivers,
Waterproof hats for deep-sea divers!

Wedding hats for the mother-in-law,
And a bobble hat that lifts as you snore!

Did some hats
catch your
attention?
Or were there
some we failed
to mention?

But, if hats look awful on your head,
Then wear a fascinator instead!